SEDUCED BY THE HOT CHEF

GAY ROMANCE

HOT AND SAUCY
BOOK FOUR

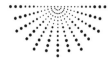

DILLON HART

CHAPTER ONE

TREY

I've ridden my Harley all over North America – across the Golden Gate Bridge, the Brooklyn Bridge, and even the Seven Mile Bridge down to the Florida Keys. I've been so far north in Canada that the roads dead-ended at permafrost. To the south, I've ridden all the way through Mexico and Central America until I reached the Darien Gap, where I laughed at the highway and decided to pull up abruptly rather than challenge that impenetrable jungle.

I've ridden across the lowest point in Death Valley and over the tallest paved roads through the Rockies. I've outrun tornadoes on the plains and woven my way down crowded Lombard Street in San Francisco.

But despite obliterating the speed limit in all forty-eight contiguous United States, I always come back to one stretch of road as my favorite.

"The Loneliest Highway in America," A.K.A. U.S. Route 50 runs east and west right through the middle of my home state, Nevada.

It's admittedly not the most scenic road in the world, unless you're a fan of sagebrush and desolation. But there's beauty in that emptiness, that same barrenness. Vast acreage uninterrupted by any sign of humanity, just mountains and desert as far as the eye can see.

I love it.

It calls to me, to that wild part of my soul that wants vast space and high speed and to leave the world behind.

It's home to me, the Nevada you can't see from the Las Vegas Strip, even from the top of the Stratosphere Tower. I'm talking about places like Eureka, Hawthorne, Goldfield, Austin, and my hometown— Tonopah. It's a few hours north of Vegas.

Tonopah's famous for three things: a turquoise mine, a haunted hotel, and being home to the founding Big Hogs Trip U motorcycle club.

Sure, having our headquarters in Tonopah is out of the way for the rest of my motorcycle club, the Triple U's, but it's also off the radar of law enforcement, just the way we like it. And besides, with chapters in Las Vegas, Reno, Sacramento, and scattered around Southern

California, you could do worse for a centralized location.

I'm Trey Hale, the reigning president of the Big Hog Triple U Motorcycle Club. Those three U's in our name stand for Unpredictable, Untamed, and Unrepentant.

Just the way I like it.

The club was founded by soldiers returning from the Korean War. Those guys are all gone now, but we have a handful of Vietnam vets who still get out and ride with us and pull their weight in whatever way the club needs.

We currently have members doing time in prisons in eleven states, mostly out west, but we have a brother on death row in Pennsylvania and two Triple U's in a supermax in Kansas.

Life on the road can be tough.

I took over a few years ago in the aftermath of a bloody turf war with the Devil's Stepchildren, a motorcycle club based in Fresno. When the dust settled, our previous president, Wayne Sutton, was among nine Triple U brothers who'd made the ultimate sacrifice for the club.

We never got an accurate body count, but I believe the Stepchildren lost twice that many. Hell, I dug holes myself out near Gabbs, Nevada, for four of them.

And that was during the annual tarantula migration.

Just sayin'.

Not much scares me, but I'm not a fan of hairy spiders the size of dinner plates.

No thanks. Hard pass.

When we met in our Las Vegas clubhouse to reorganize after losing Wayne, I was elected as his replacement, with the stipulation that the club would get out of the drug business entirely, both distribution and transport.

It's too dangerous a game, despite the big money rewards. We'd still move guns and other merchandise you can't just call your UPS man to ship for you, but drugs and dealing with the cartels was over.

I'm no Pollyanna, but I drew the line.

Didn't get into this life to destroy other people's lives with drugs, and I'm not dying over a bag of powdered junk. I don't care how much it's worth.

When I proposed that shift, I was naturally met with resistance. Guys still needed to earn, and without that cartel cash, some of them had no idea how to do it.

My suggestion? Rather than use my chain of bars and BBQ restaurants simply as money-laundering fronts, why not pump some money into them and make them profitable as what they were intended to be?

Sure, they started as vehicles for my little hot sauce hobby, but marketed correctly, and managed properly, they could be the legitimate, legal source of cashflow the Triple U's desperately needed.

Not used to getting your brisket from an outlaw biker?

I get it, but just try a bite – make sure you get a good, saucy chunk – and I bet you'll be back for more.

It's the best BBQ west of Texas, that's for sure.

And authentic as hell. There's not a man, woman, or child alive who doesn't love it.

Our Tonopah location is the smallest in the chain – after all, there are barely 2,500 people in the entire town – but even if every other location of *Hale's Beef, Bikes, and Brews* goes belly up, I'll still be behind the bar in Tonopah slinging suds and sauce.

I'd been in Ely visiting a friend, a semi-retired pilot facing a tough health diagnosis he wasn't going to bounce back from.

I spent a few days with him before riding solo from Ely to Fallon to get some wind on my face and clear my head.

Two Triple U's from Sacramento and one from Reno meet me there to ride south to Tonopah together. There have been rumors that a few renegade Devil's Stepchildren may still be flying the flag and looking for payback. Some people just don't know when a cause is lost.

Anyway, safety in numbers and all that.

We roll into Tonopah, revving our engines to announce our arrival. By the time we park and walk into Hale's, Gwen the bartender had four shots already set up for us.

It's late morning, and nobody is in the place except for a couple of old locals, dusty miners getting lubricated before heading out into the hills later in the day to look for something shiny.

We have a second round and the two Sacramento brothers hit on Gwen, which is a waste of time. She's into girls, but they don't know that, and I'm not going to mess up her tips by telling them.

Besides, even if I did, knowing those horny bastards, they'd probably just throw more money at her in the hopes of getting into some 3-way action with her and another woman. Reno and I (yeah, his name is Reno and he's from Reno. Guess my old man could have named me Tony. Tony from Tonopah? Nah, I'd have had to go by a middle name or nickname. Trey suits me fine.) went in back to wake up the cook and get some chicken wings going.

When we popped back out into the bar, Reno realizes he's made a bet the night before and never caught wind of the outcome. One problem with Tonopah is the world's worst cell service.

"Hey, Gwen, you get ESPN on any of those TVs?" he asks. "Gotta see the score of that Nuggets game last night."

"What, you don't like *Joe with the Joes?*" Gwen fires back. She has on that awful morning show, the one hosted by the two women named Joey and Josie who guzzle coffee for an hour and interview authors and B-list celebrities.

"That blonde could polish my knob anytime!" one of the Sacramento slobs hollers out, referring to the younger of the two hosts. I think she's Joey. I can never remember.

Gwen rolls her eyes and reaches for the remote. Just as she points it at the television, I glance up.

"Hey!" I snap. "Stop!"

Everybody turns and looks at me like I'd lost my mind.

Well, shit.

"Is that TV in the office working?" I ask, stepping to the end of the bar. Gwen nods.

"What channel is that?" I ask.

"Let me check," Gwen replies, clicking the remote. "314."

As I turn to head for the office, I hear the older co-host, the brunette named Joey (I think), announcing their next guest:

"After the break, we'll head over to the kitchen to chat with the brains behind the hottest barbecue sauce on the market, *Uncle Waylon's*. Surprise, he's not the grizzly old man pictured on the bottle!"

I glance back up at the screen one last time. He's no grizzled old geezer alright. I haven't seen him in what seems like a hundred years, but in reality, it has only been four. Yet there he is, looking dynamite like he always did. He smiles and waves to the camera as the studio audience claps and cheers.

The only guy who'd ever said no to me. The one that not only got away, the one that disappeared off the face of the Earth.

Laurent Grant.

Laurent fucking Grant.

I had to reach down and adjust my cock in my jeans as my mind wanders back to him.

Can't even think his name without popping a fucking boner.

It's uncomfortable getting an unexpected erection sometimes.

Especially one straight from the worst hell – and the sweetest torment – of your past.

CHAPTER TWO

LAURENT

The red light on the camera goes dark and I exhale. I can't believe how nervous I am, but hey, it is *national* television, after all.

Josie Simmons, one of the hosts, wanders over to the kitchen part of the set while Joey, her co-host, has her hair and makeup touched up by the crew.

"Nervous?" she asks.

"Yeah, just a little," I admit, trying to flash my best professional smile.

"You'll do fine. And if you're really nervous, have one of Joey's *special* coffees." She leans in close.

"They're mostly Kahlua. With a splash of bourbon. Barely any coffee," she confesses.

"Thanks," I grin. "I may need some of that. Minus the coffee and Kahlua!"

Josie laughs and reaches out to put her hand on my forearm. "Just breathe. The audience here wants to love you, they want to laugh. Just be yourself. I can't wait to try some of this." She waves her arm in the direction of the food I'd prepared.

My company has seen a modest spike in sales just since the previous Friday, when *Joe with the Joes* was announcing their guests for the upcoming week and mentioned that the founder of *Uncle Waylon's* was coming in. I couldn't wait to see the numbers in the days after the show. I hope Josie posts picture on her Instagram with one of my bottles and some sort of flowery caption about how delicious it was.

That's the social media equivalent of printing money right there.

"Thirty seconds!" calls one of the producers, and Joey gets up and saunters over toward me. She smells like a brewery.

"3-2-1 and..." The producer points at us and the red light springs to life atop the nearby camera.

"Welcome back, we've moved over to the kitchen," Joey Allenspach, ever the professional despite the daily gallons of caffeine and alcohol she consumes on-set, says with her trademark smile. "If any of you have been in the sauce aisle at your local grocery store lately, you've probably noticed the green and orange bottles you see here. They're *Uncle Waylon's*, and as the bottle says, they're 'purveyors of the finest sauces and salsas on the planet'. I have three bottles going at home right now, and I bet many of you do, too."

Josie takes over. "I just finished my last bottle, Joey! I hope they let me take some of this home today!" She laughs, and the studio audience laughs with her as if on command. "But if you're like me, you probably assumed the person behind *Uncle Waylon's* was, well, somebody's Uncle Waylon. Am I right?"

"Naturally!" Joey answers.

"Wrong!" Josie corrects. "The mad scientist who comes up with all these concoctions, the sauces and salsas and rubs and all of it, isn't anybody's uncle. In fact, he's barely reached adulthood! For the first time, please welcome Mister Will Laughlin to *Joe with the Joes!*"

I smile and clutch at the counter in an effort to keep my hands from shaking quite so much.

"Thank you, everyone," I say as the applause dies down.

"Okay, so of course my first question is, who is Uncle Waylon?" Joey asks.

I laugh and take a deep breath.

"He's right here," I say, picking up a bottle of hot sauce and pointing to the cartoon sketch of the angry man on the front of every bottle.

"Is he a real person?" Josie asks, her smile going a little tighter. I remind myself I have to flow with this conversational direction, whether I like it or not.

This is the promotional opportunity of a lifetime.

"No," I admit. "But he's the face of the company. The mascot, I suppose. I don't even know anybody named Waylon, except Waylon Jennings. But the marketing department thought we needed somebody people could recognize. A *Ronald McDonald*. And I thought putting a college kid's face, my face, on the bottle might cause macho men to look elsewhere for their BBQ sauce."

"Oh, honey, I'd fire that marketing department," Joey chirps. "If I had your face to look at on the bottle, Arnold and I would have your sauce on everything, including our breakfast cereal. I'd insist."

Arnold is her husband, who she references at least seven hundred times on each broadcast, usually with regard to how he couldn't keep his hands off her despite being unable to keep his eyes and mind off other women.

"Well, getting rid of the marketing department might be a little tricky," I counter. "Since I'm it."

Everyone laughs. My nerves begin to dissipate.

"I came up with Uncle Waylon at my kitchen table. And my best friend drew the original sketch that became our logo."

"And the recipes for all this deliciousness?" Josie asks. "Is it true that they're yours?"

"Every last one of them," I respond. "They represent hundreds of hours of experimentation and research. Trial and error. God bless the guinea pigs who had to eat some of my early efforts."

I never poisoned anybody, to my knowledge, but I could admit that, along the way, some of my stuff was borderline inedible.

"It was just you at home in your kitchen working on this stuff?" Josie asks. "Did your wife or kids or anybody else help?"

"No, really just me," I said. "I'm single."

"Whoa!" Joey shrieks. "Hear that Josie? He's single. You're not! Don't get any ideas!" Everyone laughs again, on cue.

"What's been your most popular product?" Josie asks.

"Without a doubt, this one," I replied, reaching for the large bottle on the end. "*Trey's Big Hog Smoky BBQ Sauce.* It's not our hottest, but it has that... smoky, robust flavor, and then right when it almost overwhelms you, it has this great kick, right at the end."

"I want to try Trey's *Big Hog*," Joey says with a wink. Josie rolls her eyes.

"I've got some wings here that were tossed with just a little sea salt and brown sugar. They'll be great with some *Trey's*," I suggest, lifting the tray and angling it toward the two hosts. A dish filled with *Trey's* sits nearby.

"I can't wait," Jodie says. "And we're going to pass some out to the studio audience to try as well." The producer signals several assistants to begin passing out trays with a couple wings each, accompanied by small containers of *Trey's*. "In the meantime, tell us about it. Where did you come up with the idea? With the name?"

"Well, I can't give up too much, but I've experimented with a smoker using all sorts of different types of wood and combinations, and you name the peppers and I've probably at the very least tried them, if not used them, in one or more of my recipes.

"This particular combination though? The first time I tried it on chicken, I knew it was a keeper."

"Is Trey fictional like Waylon?" Josie asked.

"Umm," I begin, fighting the urge to squirm. "Not exactly."

"Oh, do tell," Joey asks, leaning in. I glance over at Josie, who is inhaling wings. Evidently, she likes it. My hopes of an Instagram shout-out are bolstered.

"I knew a guy named Trey years ago in Las Vegas," I explain, waving a hand vaguely and castigating myself for not having come up with a better story.

"And he was a pig farmer?" Joey asks, eyes twinkling. "Or does that *Hog* in the name refer to something else that was big?"

Josie shoots her a look. The deeper into a show she gets, the more drunk and inappropriate Joey becomes.

"Well, he was a biker," I explain. "And he rode a Harley, so the name just kind of fell into place."

"Was this Trey a special friend?" Josie asks between bites. "I mean, to name a sauce after someone they must be pretty special. And who doesn't love a man on a Harley, am I right?"

The women in the audience cheer. The men just keep gobbling their chicken wings, pretending not to understand the innuendo.

Have you ever tried not to blush? I mean really *tried* not to blush? Yeah, it has the opposite effect. Sigh. So, I blush a deep crimson, even with all the makeup they'd caked on me before throwing me in front of a camera.

"Trey was…" I began but lost my train of thought. Well, I didn't *lose* it so much as the train stopped at a station that was entirely inappropriate for network television. Thinking too long about Trey Hale inevitably took me to his forearms... and the way his biceps stretched his t-shirts... and his *bulge*.

So, I freeze.

Blushing red as a radish, live on national television, staring into space, with my mouth hanging open and my tongue gently touching my top lip, my pulse racing with visions of Trey Hale's dick *moving* in his jeans.

My mind goes back to before.

We are sitting in the breakroom at the restaurant where we work together, talking and flirting, and when he stands up and turns to reach for his motorcycle helmet his crotch is right there, a foot away from my face, and his dick shifts in his pants on its own accord. It has to be my imagination, but I swear it throbbed.

Yeah.

And then think about that kiss...

"Will, I have to tell you, this *Big Hog* sauce is one of the best things I've ever put in my mouth!" Joey declares. She is so drunk it is a wonder she is still upright. Her comment snaps me out of my X-rated, badly timed reverie.

"Oh, wonderful, great, I'm glad you like it!" I say, forcing a big smile.

They go to a commercial, and when we return the segment concludes with me giving some basic recipes for ribs and brisket, with my sauces and rubs figuring prominently.

Josie wraps things up solo, as Joey had disappeared backstage during the commercial and never returned. I guessed that she'd passed out.

"Will Laughlin and his *Uncle Waylon's* line of sauces will be competing next month in Las Vegas at the annual *Sin City Blazin' Hot Chili Cookoff,* televised live on our sister show, *Eat This!* So, make sure to tune in. Check local listings. And everybody in the studio audience, plus ten lucky winners from Twitter, will be taking home a gift basket of *Uncle Waylon's* products today!" The audience goes wild. The wings had been a huge hit, and backstage Josie tells me they'd love to have me back again.

Once I am alone, I finally let out a deep breath I felt like I'd been holding for an hour.

No matter where I run to, Trey Hale is never far from my mind.

CHAPTER THREE

TREY

The television in the office is old and small and doesn't have near the picture the big flat screens out in the bar do, but I want to be alone while I watch.

I shut the door, settle behind the desk, and punch up 314 on the remote.

A car commercial ends, then one for diapers, and finally a trailer for a romantic comedy that includes a hot air balloon with a bunch of puppies in it for some reason.

Finally, the *Joe with the Joes* show returns, the camera swinging from the cheering studio audience around past the couches and over to a small kitchen area before zooming in on the older of the two co-hosts.

Her eyes are so glazed I'd have bet she is drunk, but she's on TV so I figure that can't be the case.

She and her co-host banter for a minute before they turn their attention to the man standing behind them – Laurent Grant.

I stared at the screen as they discussed his barbecue sauce, its logo and branding, blah blah blah.

I'd tried the stuff, and it was good. Damn good.

Laurent is Uncle Waylon? The hell you say.

He and I had had a... well, what we had really just amounted to a moment. A kiss. A single kiss that I thought... expected... hoped would be more.

But in the end, that's all it was. And then he was gone.

Not just gone, but *gone*, as in completely incognito. Phone turned off, social media closed, vanished. I even had our guy Randolph, and he's damn good – he can normally find anything or anyone –look for him, and he couldn't find him.

Now here he is. Looking as gorgeous as ever.

His hair was even thicker than I remember, auburn and wavy. Every inch of those muscles shown to good effect in the upscale outfit he wears. Fewer freckles than I remembered him having, but I figure that could be makeup for TV.

He and the two hosts chat about his sauces and rubs and salsas and all that shit, and even though he seems nervous at first, he relaxes and the interview flows. He is a natural.

Except they called him… *Will Laughlin?* I have no doubt in my mind he is Laurent Grant. Nobody other man is that beautiful. And hearing his voice confirms it. But the fact that he has a different name made sense. If he was still going by Laurent Grant, my guy Randolph would have found him. Even with a new name, he should have found him. Unless the feds made sure his name change wasn't filed the way they usually are. Even so…

I have a lot to think about, but I can't peel my eyes away from the screen or my ears away from his melodic voice.

The audience is laughing, the co-hosts seem to love his food, and I marvel at him and his success. I pull my laptop out of my bag and punch up the *Uncle Waylon's* site. I poke around and find a brief "Our story" section. It details the business starting on a kitchen table in Santa Fe, New Mexico. The company is now headquartered near Knoxville, Tennessee.

My attention is split between my laptop and the television until I hear my name.

One of the hosts asks Laurent which product is most popular, and he replies, "Without a doubt, this one."

He picks up a large bottle from the end of the display in front of him. "*Trey's Big Hog Smoky BBQ Sauce.* It's not our hottest, but it has that... smoky, robust flavor, and then right when it almost overwhelms you, it has this great kick, right at the end."

They continue, and my name flies around the studio, and as Laurent describes the man who inspired the sauce – Las Vegas, rode a Harley – there's no doubt he meant me.

One of the hosts asks him if "Trey" had been some kind of special friend, and Laurent freezes.

He stares at the camera like the proverbial deer in headlights, his mouth just barely moving, trying to form words. It is an awkward moment, to be sure, but the way his mouth hung open made me want to... well. I need to reach down and adjust myself before my erection goes from half-mast to full.

I haven't thought much about Laurent lately, or at least he no longer consumes my thoughts as he once did, but seeing him like this, on television, talking, laughing, looking better than ever. Things begin to stir inside me.

Feelings I'd buried, desire I'd tried to move past. Tried and failed, evidently.

To call Laurent Grant "the one who got away" would be missing the big picture – he had been the only one who ever said no.

Not only that, but in a sense, he'd been the one mountain I'd never climbed in a lifetime of reaching every summit I ever set my mind to cresting.

Growing up in little Tonopah, Nevada, from a young age I was always the tallest, the strongest, the fastest, and the best at any and every sport or game I played. I got straight A's with little effort.

Once I hit middle school, however, my focus changed.

I grew up without a father, my dad deciding not to stick around once my teenage mother gave birth to me. I have a picture of a man holding an infant that my grandmother says is him. On the back somebody wrote in blue ink, "Richie and Trey" and a date that was four days after I was born.

He's burly and shirtless, with long, scraggly dark hair and a wide smile behind a thick bushy beard and mustache combo. He has tattoos on his chest that are tough to make out, and you can't really see his eyes as he's looking down at what he's holding in his arms – an infant screaming and swinging his arms in a blue onesie.

All I've ever known about this mysterious "Richie" guy is that he fathered me, hung around for a little while, then vanished. Hale, the last name I use, came from my mom.

On my birth certificate it lists my mother as Rhonda Hale. The father space is blank. When I was old enough to realize it was unusual not to at least know who your father is, I asked my grandmother and others who might know. I hit a brick wall.

"He's a bad man," and "Best to let that sleeping dog lie," were typical responses.

It's not like my mother could be of any help; she spent most of our brief time together strung out on whatever drugs or alcohol she could get her hands on. She wasn't picky; she'd drink motor oil if she thought it could get her drunk, and if you put a pill in front of her she'd take it, no questions asked.

By the time I was seven, and she was twenty-three, she was gone.

My grandmother, a blackjack dealer at one of the smoky, depressing local casinos, took me in. When I went looking for a father figure, it was my Uncle Russell who stepped in. Rhonda's older brother by five years, Russell had done a stint in the Army before winding up in Las Vegas and hooking up with the Triple U's.

I went from riding a Big Wheel to a bicycle to tearing up and down desert highways on a Harley by the time I was fourteen.

All I ever wanted was to get my own patch and join the club. I was already Unpredictable and Untamed; now I just needed something to be Unrepentant about.

CHAPTER FOUR

LAURENT

It has been more than four years since I last set foot in Las Vegas, but here I am, entering in the *Sin City Blazin' Hot Chili Cookoff*, smack dab on Las Vegas Boulevard.

The television exposure alone is worth the trip, but I plan to win. I considered sending some trusted employees in my stead; after all, when I left Las Vegas I swore to never return.

But I'd been keeping up with the local news, and between what was reported there and what my best friend Tanya's FBI cousin tells her, the biker wars of a few years ago are over.

With the runaway success of the business I'd launched two years ago, I'd had to come out of my pseudo-

Witness Protection Program lifestyle more and more, and everything has been fine. The final step toward becoming a full-fledged public figure had been appearing on national TV. I have to believe there is nobody left out there looking to use me to get to Trey Hale.

It's the only way that I can get on with my life, and it's time to do just that.

As if he cared more about me than being another notch on his belt anyway.

We'd worked together for a couple years and, yeah, of course I was attracted to him. Have you seen him? A body sculpted from granite, covered in leather, topped off by a square jaw and ice blue eyes? Hel-lo!

But we were never a *thing*. I had a crush on him. Of course. Like everybody else who saw him did. But we never even hooked up. He was into girls anyway, those easy groupie kinds of girls – way too much makeup, hair teased up to the sky, as little clothing as they could get away with; you know the type. Lots of fake boobs and, nowadays, fake butts, too.

I was a basic small town boy at best; I didn't stand a chance of competing with those women.

Yeah, I got it, I was never going to be a guy like Trey Hale's type. I had the wrong plumbing, for one thing. Even if there were rumors about him hooking up with men, they weren't men like me and I was pretty much a goody goody two shoes to boot. Plus I wasn't exactly male model material anyway. That's one of the drawbacks of working in the food industry – you're around food all the time. And some of it, or too much of it, inevitably winds up inside you. Not to mention long hours, stress, and too much exhaustion to spend much time in the gym.

And yeah, my figure wound up a bit fuller than a biker stud like Trey Hale was after.

But the one thing I had to cling to was that kiss. There was no denying that. Maybe he kissed every lover like that, but I'd never been kissed like that. It was hot and passionate and deep and when it was over, I was gasping for air while my heart pounded out of my chest.

Okay, maybe I spend a little too much time thinking about it. But if you've ever been kissed like that, even once, I bet you remember it vividly.

But just when that kiss was undoubtedly going to turn into more, his phone buzzed. And whatever or whoever was on the other end of that buzz was more important than me, so off he went, leaving me in that alley behind the restaurant, wondering what just happened.

Once I composed myself, and the roar of his Harley disappearing down the street told me it wasn't worth waiting around hoping for more, I walked across the street to grab a soda and snack for later.

That short walk was just enough time for the ambush to be set up.

I walked back around the building toward my car, a Mr. Pibb in one hand and a bag with Cheetos and an ice cream sandwich in the other, when I was grabbed and shoved up against the wall by two guys in masks.

Just thinking about it now makes me want to throw up as I struggle to keep from going into a full-blown panic attack.

"I have cash, I have money in my backpack, please don't hurt me," I remember babbling into their masked faces, my eyes frantically searching the empty air behind them for help.

"Shut up!" the larger man commanded. "Scream and I'll gut you."

I hadn't even realized there was a knife until that point, but he held it up and it glinted from the streetlight. It was big and wouldn't take any expertise or much effort to go right through me.

The second guy leaned in close. "You're Trey Hale's little bitch, right?"

I was? No, I wasn't. I mean, yeah, I wished I was his... *something*. But whatever being an "little bitch" entailed, I didn't think I was it.

I shook my head frantically.

"Yeah you are," the larger man said. "He'll want you back. No doubt."

My mind spun a million miles per hour.

What the fuck was going on?

Trey was a biker, in a motorcycle gang, I knew that. He wore a patch and he had scary-looking friends who wore the same vests and patches. I'm not dumb; I know a gang when I see one. Their vests and jackets all had the same insignia, "UUU," all curling down into a handle like a fancy trident or pitchfork.

"Come on," the bigger guy said, grabbing my upper arm with a vise grip and basically dragging me across the parking lot. I forced my eyes to focus, to try to glean some details; I knew that was important.

If I was being abducted or something, I needed every crumb of information I could get, and knowing it was two guys, one with a knife, wearing ski masks, wasn't enough.

The smaller guy, walking ahead, had on a leather vest. Like the one Trey wore, but not with the same name or patches on it.

It said "Devils" across the top, then a sinister, sneering face in the middle. There was a word at the bottom, but I couldn't make it out.

For the first time, I saw the van. It was running, I don't know how I missed hearing it. The side door was wide open.

Never let them take you to a secondary location!

I'd taken a self-defense class and watched enough episodes of *Criminal Minds* and other shows like it to know that much.

So, I started to struggle. When the big burly knife guy took his next step, I planted my foot and swung the other one as hard as I could, kicking straight up between his legs and hoping for the best.

He yelped and collapsed to the concrete, his partner spinning to see what all the ruckus was about. I tried to turn and run, but fear took over and it was like trying to run through syrup. My arms and legs moved in slow motion as I hyperventilated.

The second guy was on me in a heartbeat, knocking me to the ground.

"Bad idea, faggot," he growled in my ear. "We don't give a shit about you, just your boyfriend. But now you're in it, too."

He yanked me to my feet, and I deflated. The first guy was already on his feet, and the driver of the van got out and came around. "What the fuck, Diesel? Get that fruit in the van and let's go!"

The first guy grabbed me again, harder this time, and they lifted me off the ground as I kicked futilely.

We were a step away from the van when I heard a *crack* and I found myself on the ground.

The smaller guy was on the ground, and the larger one was being attacked.

I rolled over to find a guy with long blond hair wildly swinging a baseball bat at my abductors. He wore a UUU vest.

I'd seen him around once or twice with Trey, but I'd never met him.

He connected with the bat to the head of the larger masked man, and he fell into the open van. The smaller guy got up and tackled Trey's friend and they scuffled on the ground. I managed to scoot away from the melee on my bottom, shaking with terror.

The Triple U biker was getting the upper hand when the driver of the van came around the front of the van with a shotgun in his hands.

"Behind you!" I screamed, and Trey's friend swung around, catching the barrel of the shotgun with the bat just as it discharged.

The sound was deafening.

As three men now scuffled, I realized I was just a few feet away from my car and my backpack was close enough to reach. I snatched it up and somehow got behind the wheel of my car and pulled out of the parking lot in a panicked daze.

I have no recollection of how I got there, but I wound up at Tanya's condo, pounding on her door.

I couldn't think of anywhere else to go. I didn't feel safe going home or going back to work or anywhere but Tanya's. Her boyfriend worked as a bouncer; he was big and tough, and she had mentioned an uncle or cousin or something who was in the FBI.

That night, Tanya drove me to Phoenix in her car, straight through, stopping only for gas and coffee. Every time a motorcycle passed us, I sank down low and hid.

Her cousin was an FBI agent in the Phoenix, Arizona field office, and he was a godsend.

Two days later, I was in a safe house in Knoxville, Tennessee, being debriefed by a joint task force of FBI agents and Las Vegas Metro police. I was shown a series of pictures, one of whom was the guy with long, blond hair who rescued me. His name was Tick McDonough, and he'd been a member of the Triple U MC. He was now dead. Along with three members of a rival motorcycle club, the Devil's Stepchildren.

Somehow, I'd escaped as the first shots were fired in a gang war. Since nobody but me survived that day, and since I was ruled out as a suspect in the quadruple homicide, there was no reason for me to return to Las Vegas to testify in any trial.

I didn't sleep for three months afterward without chemical assistance, and lots of it.

There was no way I was going back to Las Vegas. Even Trey Hale wasn't handsome enough to get me in the middle of a war between rival motorcycle gangs.

I'd start a new life somewhere else. Maybe I'd try what Trey had often suggested and try to bottle my sauces and sell them myself.

CHAPTER FIVE

TREY

The show ends, and I click the remote, shutting the television off. I lean back in my chair and look at the ceiling.

Laurent Grant is alive after all. Even though he is now apparently Will Laughlin.

I have another piece of the puzzle, but it is a center piece, not much use without all the edges. Truth is, I'm woefully short of those.

"Hey, boss, everything okay?" Reno says through the door after rapping on it.

"Yeah, bro. But hey, come on in."

Reno comes in and sits down across the desk from me and shrugs.

"Think back four years ago," I open. "A little farther back than that, actually. Remember when Tick got killed?"

"Shit yeah," Reno replies. "Took out a bunch of Stepchildren with him, right?"

"Three of them," I confirm. "He was a fucking badass."

"What's making you bring him up?"

"That night, I don't know if you caught wind of this, but there was a guy... I worked at the restaurant where the whole thing with Tick went down. This guy I worked with, we were getting... *close*, you know?"

Reno raises his eyebrow. "Interesting. Anybody I know?"

"No," I reply, shaking my head. "Don't think you ever met him. He didn't run with our crowd. Anyway, that night, the night Tick was killed, this guy and I, his name was Laurent, Laurent and I were out back in that parking lot, just the two of us. We were getting to know one another a little bit."

Reno gives me a confused look. Triple U had gay memebers, but as far as Reno knew, I wasn't one of them. Plus Triple U members, like those of most motorcycle clubs, don't typically go through what would be considered the "normal" courtship stuff like going on dates or making out like teenagers. We usually see somebody we like and they're either into our lifestyle or they aren't, and if they are, we hook up. That's just the way it works.

But Laurent is different, and I find myself frustrated that I have to explain.

"He wasn't my bitch. He wasn't that type. He was different. Way too good for me, but I was in there giving it my best shot. Whatever developed between us, it was a slow burn. He was guarded. He had this wall, but I was drawn to him. Couldn't help myself."

I stop and picture Laurent in my head, little things like when he'd wear a shirt that just barely reached to his pants and he'd reach or twist a certain way and it would ride up and I'd get just a glimpse of the small of his back or his happy trail. For some reason that V shape that his hips formed was sexier than going to a strip club with the guys and seeing what were, by any measure, very attractive girls getting completely naked. They just weren't in Laurent's class. He was pure, he was something I couldn't touch, couldn't even see, which made me want him all the more.

He was an angel.

"Okay I'm just going to come out and say it. We were kissing back there. First time we'd kissed. I didn't know where it was going, what it could become, but I'd have been happy back there kissing him and smelling his hair for the rest of the night.

"But I got a phone call, and it was Wayne, and he needed me."

"Hey, brother, the prez calls, you go. No questions asked," Reno comments. I nod, though it hadn't been easy to walk away that night.

"So, yeah, it sucked, but I left. I apologized to Laurent, told him I'd call him later to check on him, hopefully to resume what we'd been doing, but either way, Wayne called, so I went. He needed me to meet him out in Boulder City, out by the dam. He had some business going down and he needed backup, needed me and a bunch of brothers out there to fly the flag."

Reno nods, listening intently.

"I rode out, there were fifteen of us out there, he was meeting some Loco Lobos out there and he wanted to have some muscle there just in case.

"The whole thing didn't take long, and we rode back into town and planned to stop at *Champagne Charlie's* to get good and drunk. I just wanted to catch up with Laurent, but you didn't say no to Wayne.

"We were just pulling in when my phone lit up, so did Wayne's. We both had guys on Metro, and they were calling to tell us about Mick and see what we knew.

"Wayne and I went over there to the scene and I noticed Laurent's car was gone when we got there. I asked the detective if they knew anything about a a redhead college kid and they said no, but that they had security footage from that store across the street and they'd let me know.

"Tick was gone, but he took three Stepchildren with him."

"He was a tough motherfucker," Reno notes, and I nod in agreement.

"I scrapped with him once over cards. Getting punched by him was like being hit by a truck. I was sure he was wearing brass knuckles or something when we fought, but no, that was just him."

Reno laughs and rubs his jaw, wincing at the memory of being punched by Tick McDonough. He'd had his own run-ins with Tick. Everybody had. Tick had the shortest temper of anybody I ever knew, but when shit went down there was nobody you wanted by your side more than him.

"We rounded everybody up and got things as sorted out as we could," I say, "You remember, you got the call."

"Shit yes," Reno recalls. "I was up near Boise making a run with two other brothers and then we got word about Tick and to get our guards up, to get armed and get ready. We didn't know what was coming next."

I nod. "That night, I went with Wayne and Hatchet and we met with the president of the local Devil's Stepchildren chapter up on top of the Stratosphere Tower. Just the six of us up there to hash things out. I don't know if you've ever heard this part, but we're up there, neutral ground, you know, and they're coming up on the elevator, just about to reach the top, and I get a call from my detective; he'd just watched the surveillance tape from the gas station.

"Laurent had walked over there right after I left, and as soon as he crossed back over, two guys in masks grabbed him. Then they went out of view, but just after that, Tick rolled up and parked out front. He went around the corner with a bat in hand, and all hell broke loose.

"The tape showed Laurent's car come flying out right after, but you couldn't see who was driving. And that's it. Last time anybody saw or heard from Laurent Grant. Until today. Just now."

"You got all that with the Stepchildren brass coming for a meet?"

"Yeah," I nod. "And I was hot. I was ready to throw that fat bastard president of theirs, D.D., off the tower and his two lieutenants with him. But Wayne wanted to keep the peace as long as we could, so they talked it over.

"D.D. claimed he didn't have any idea what was happening, pleaded ignorance up and down the board, which I knew was bullshit, but we couldn't prove anything yet, either.

"Right after they left, Wayne turned me loose to go check on Laurent. I started calling him, checked his house, nothing. I talked to my guy at Metro, but they came up empty, too."

"That's why you were so ruthless during the war with that scum," Reno says, looking a little shocked.

"Yep. I figured one of them had to know something, so I'd just keep beating them until one of them gave it up. Every chance I got, I worked them for information. But I got nowhere.

"Eventually, I came to believe that one of them had made some sort of connection between him and I, and that he was an innocent bystander, caught in the cross-fire. A casualty of war. I never dreamed I'd see him again, especially on national television."

"That's some wild shit, brother," Reno says, leaning back in his chair. "So, where is he? What's the play?"

"That's just it. I don't know what the play is exactly, or necessarily where he is, but he's coming to us. One of the reasons he was on the show is because he's coming to Las Vegas next month for the chili cookoff." I try to ignore the tightening in my chest, and the twitching of my cock, at the thought of seeing Laurent again.

"Not the one at Hale's, right?"

"Wrong. Absolutely the one at our place. The one I intend to win. I just never considered that I'd have to beat him to do it."

CHAPTER SIX

LAURENT

❖

After everything went down in Vegas, I was reborn as Will Laughlin in a version of witness protection. I am evidently a "high-value target," according to the FBI, or the Stepchildren wouldn't have risked an abduction like that in public.

They suggested I enter "The Program," that I adopt a new identity, go somewhere nobody knew me, and forget all about Las Vegas and anybody I knew there.

I'd lived in Vegas since just after I graduated high school. Everybody and mostly everything I knew was there, but it was time to close that chapter of my life and begin anew.

After all, it's not like I hadn't had practice.

Before Las Vegas, I'd grown up in Jacksonville, Florida, with a brief stop in Santa Fe, New Mexico. I had a normal childhood, lots of trips to the beach, I played basketball, I was as happy as can be. My junior year, I was named to the all-district basketball team and my school made it to the state quarterfinals, deeper than we'd ever gone before.

College coaches had noticed me, and I was starting to get some interest. No official scholarship offers, but with a strong summer and solid senior year, it seemed like I could get college paid for. My family didn't struggle financially, but hey, college is expensive. A scholarship, even partial, would be a godsend.

That all changed two weeks after my junior year of high school ended.

My best friend Rachel had just dropped me off at home after a day at the beach. My skin had that hot, burnt, sun-kissed feeling, and I was exhausted. I got in the shower, but while I was in there, I heard a loud crash over the sound of the water. Loud enough to startle me. I stuck my head through the curtain. "Dad? Is everything okay?"

"Bear, lock the door! Stay in there!" he shouted, running down the hallway past the bathroom.

He always called me Bear, a nickname I didn't let anybody else use. It's what he had called me since I was a baby

I'd never heard him use that tone of voice; I was terrified.

I got out, dripping wet, and locked the door, wrapping a towel around my body and using another to quickly dry my hair.

Voices I didn't recognize came from the other side of the door – angry, male voices. "Where did that little shit go? Check in there. He has a wife and kid; round them all up!"

Then I heard the doorknob jiggling.

If it's possible to be scared to death, I was right on the brink just then.

I didn't know it then, but the worst was yet to come.

Bang! Bang! Bang!

Gunshots rang out, which I wouldn't have even recognized as such, but what else could they be? I'd never seen a gun except in the movies, much less heard one fired so close to me.

More shouting. More gunshots. Another crash.

"Come on, baby Bear, we have to get out of here! Right now!"

It was my father's voice, followed by three loud knocks on the door.

"Dad? What's going on?" I was sobbing.

My quiet, normal, all-American life was over.

"Nothing, Bear, but we have to go. I have clothes for you. Come on, kid."

Just as my shaking hand reached the doorknob, I heard another gunshot, followed by my father screaming.

"Ahhhh! Motherfucker!" Then another two shots, and everything went quiet.

Too quiet.

"Daddy?" I called out but got no reply.

Eventually, I had no choice. I had to open the door.

I found my father slumped against the wall opposite the door, blood all over his shirt. I glanced down the hallway to see splintered wood, broken glass, and two bodies. They were face down, but there was blood everywhere and they weren't moving.

"Don't look at them, Bear," came my dad's voice, barely above a whisper. "Help me up. We have to get out of here. Right now."

He had one of my T shirts and a pair of basketball shorts lying next to him, the blue ones with the black and silver stripes up the sides. I rubbed my head with the towel enough to get my hair semi dry and slipped the shirt over my head.

"I don't understand... what's... Dad, you're bleeding. Please tell me what's going on!" A full-blown panic attack clawed at the edges of my mind, but I knew I couldn't surrender to it.

"They're bad guys, Laurent," he said. When he used my full name, I knew things were serious. "There's another one in the kitchen."

It was then that I noticed the gun in my father's hand, a menacing black pistol.

"Why do you have a gun?" I asked, helping him to his feet.

He got his footing and told me to grab some more towels and meet him at the back door.

The back of his shirt just had a little blood, the front a lot more. I watched him shuffle down the hallway and kick the two bodies there to verify that they didn't pose any further threat.

I grabbed towels from the bathroom and followed him.

"Don't look at them," he reiterated. "Focus on me."

His voice was weak, and he was shaking. The tanned, athletic surfer and deep-sea diver I knew as my dad had gone pale, and he looked like he'd lost forty pounds of muscle instantly as a result of the gunshot.

I followed him out the back door, where he kept peeking around corners as if expecting more trouble.

"You need a hospital," I said as we reached his car, only to find the tires flattened.

"No time for that," he countered. "Stay low. Stay here. I'll be right back."

He went back in the house and returned with a set of keys in his hand. He winced with every step and sucked in deep breaths in order to keep going.

"They must have a car nearby," he said, and I helped him to the end of the driveway. He clicked the key fob a few times and a blue SUV two doors down beeped. "You have to drive, Bear,"

"Drive where? To the hospital?"

He shook me off. "Just drive. Go toward the freeway. I'll tell you where."

I helped him lay across the backseat and I got behind the wheel. We hadn't gone a mile before he made a horrible choking sound and I sped for the nearest hospital I knew of.

He was gone by the time I saw signs for the ER.

CHAPTER SEVEN

TREY

Two weeks before the *Sin City Blazin' Hot Chili Cookoff,* producers from *Eat This!*, the cable network that would air the contest, arrived in Las Vegas to shoot some footage of the restaurant and surroundings. They also plan to do an interview with me.

The contest has been held annually for twenty-two years at various locations around Las Vegas, drawing competitors from all over the country. It's aired on *Eat This!* originally as part of a quarterly series they did about the culinary scene in Las Vegas.

Eventually they decided the contest was worthy of its own slot, which grew from a one-hour special to a series of episodes that took on more of a reality show flavor, visiting some competitors' home kitchens and talking about their road to Las Vegas.

Today they send their rising star, plus-sized model Stacia Salt, to interview me.

I hate the hot lights and the makeup they make me wear, but ever since it had been announced that the cookoff was relocating to Hale's this year, business at all our locations has been up considerably. So I am willing to put up with minor inconveniences.

"The *Sin City Blazin' Hot Chili Cookoff* is still two weeks away, but I'm already here in Las Vegas, soaking up the sun, hitting the tables, and checking out all the new restaurants in town," Stacia Salt opens, flashing a Hollywood smile at the cameras. "Speaking of new, the chili cookoff has a new home this year, but it won't be new to anybody on the west coast who likes barbecue. It's the flagship location, mid-Las Vegas Strip, of *Hale's Beef, Bikes, and Brews,* and I'm here today with the founder, Mister Trey Hale!"

"Thanks," I say. I am totally out of my element. I second-guess pretty much every word I say on camera.

I wear a black *Hale's* golf shirt for the interview and tied my hair back in a tight ponytail. The tattoos on my neck are plain to see, and according to the producers, they make me look "dangerous" and "authentic."

Whatever. I don't give a shit about looking dangerous, and I know I am authentic; to hell with the rest of it.

They are lucky I didn't insist on wearing my vest. The old-timers would have never agreed to me sitting for an interview, but if I did, they'd have insisted I fly the flag.

The old-timers loved to contradict themselves. Maybe that was why so few of them had survived long enough to retire. I don't intend to follow in their footsteps.

You can change with the times, and still stay true to your most important values.

The interview is pretty standard stuff, with Stacia prodding me to brag about my chili and how I plan to defend the championship trophy I'd won the past two years.

She asks me about our restaurants, the food we serve, our beer choices, and what my plans are for the future.

"We're happy right where we are," I reply, giving her my best grin. "We're at a good size, I think. If you're asking if I'm planning to expand nationally, or if your viewers will find our stuff in their local grocery stores, hey, none of us know what the future holds, but I wouldn't expect it anytime soon. Besides, everybody comes to Vegas or California eventually, right? So just stop in and see us."

"Do you worry that families might balk at visiting a biker bar?" she asks. "Even if it's sort of, you know, *Disneyfied?*"

I look around. "Almost all of our locations have separate sides for the bar and the restaurant, and I wouldn't expect families to spend much time at any bars, biker or otherwise," I counter. "But as far as the restaurant side, as long as your family doesn't mind good food and lots of it, bring grandma, grandpa, and all the kids."

The interview wraps up, and they finally turn the blinding lights off, thank God.

As Stacia is chatting with her producers, I tug on her sleeve. "Got a minute? Off the record?"

"Sure!" She grins. "I was hoping you'd ask."

I don't have in mind what I think she has in mind.

We went back to my office and sat down.

"How do you think it went?" I ask. "I was pretty nervous."

"You looked great, you did great, we're expecting to do big numbers for the contest. Hopefully it'll be great for your bottom line, having it here."

"And winning again," I remind her.

"Of course," she concedes, fluttering her long, fake lashes up at me.

"Have you been to see many of the other competitors?" I ask. Maybe I'm shooting too straight here, but I don't have much time before competitors land.

Before I'm face to face with Laurent, I need whatever details I can get.

"Last week I was in Odessa, Texas, to see the Fenimore brothers," she replies. They'd finished second to me last year. "And I've been around to a few others. We have a trip through California next week and then up to Reno. We won't catch everybody, but we'll have a good cross-section. According to social media, most of our viewers just want to see you, anyway."

"Pfft," I say, waving her off.

"They really want us to somehow get your shirt off," she adds, sounding a bit hopeful. "But we haven't come up with a good angle for that yet. Maybe if you win, you rip it off and twirl it over your head?"

"When," I say, and she cocks her head. "*When* I win. You said 'if'."

"Sorry, *when* you win," she is grinning like she thinks I'm being cocky.

If only she knew.

"But no," I laugh. "I don't think I'll take my shirt off like that on national television."

"How about in private?" she asks. "In my hotel suite?"

She bites her bottom lip and tries to look sexy. She doesn't have to try very hard; she is gorgeous.

But she's not my type. She isn't Laurent Grant.

And I can't get that man out of my head.

"Wouldn't that constitute a conflict of interest?" I ask, trying to defuse things without making it awkward.

"Nobody has to know," Stacia says. "I'll do *anything* you want."

The way she said "anything" made her intentions crystal clear. Any straight man not hung up on his ex, not counting the seconds until he sees him again, would have locked the door to my office and put that "anything" to the test.

But I'm uncomfortably feeling like a one-lover man – and I haven't even seen that lover in years.

I laugh as if going along with a joke, giving her the chance to gracefully let her suggestion drop.

"Have you been to see the *Uncle Waylon's* people?" I ask.

She is caught off guard by my question and composes herself for the new direction our conversation is going by clearing her throat and sitting up straight in her chair.

"*Uncle Waylon's?*" she asks, as if I'd said something in Aramaic rather than English.

I nod.

"Oh. Um, yes. Yeah, we were in Tennessee last week. Are you worried about them?"

"Well, their sauce is pretty good," I say casually. "Not sure about their chili, though."

Suddenly it hits her. *"Trey's Big Hog!* That's right. From *Joe with the Joe's!* Oh my God. I almost forgot!"

I shrug and smile.

"You and Will were... an item? Oh, that's *juicy!* Yes! What an angle. Thank you for reminding me."

"Pump the brakes; we were never an *item*. It's a long story. But we did know each other, a million years ago."

"Big Hog? Seriously? If you weren't an item, you were definitely hooking up."

"Never had the pleasure," I confess.

"He doesn't seem like your type anyway," Stacia counters.

"How would you know what my type is?" I ask with a chuckle. Just a minute ago, Stacia had thought that *she* was my type.

"You're the president of a... how do I put this... *notorious* motorcycle club," Stacia replies.

"Allegedly," I respond.

She stands up and walks over to where my vest hangs from a set of shelves. She spreads it open to reveal the Triple U trident and the "President" patch along the bottom. She held her palm flat and arched her eyebrows.

"Okay, maybe the allegations have a little bite to them," I admit, laughing.

"Ya think?" she asks, strolling over to my desk to sit on the corner, facing me. "As such, you definitely have a type. Wild and willing. Will Laughlin's idea of a sex toy would be a spatula. Not your type. But my offer still stands," she says standing up.

She gathers her blonde hair up and holds it behind her head, turning her ass in my direction. "Remember what I said. *Anything* you want."

I stand up and hold up my hands in surrender.

"I'll keep it in mind." I walk over and open my office door. "Thanks for the interview and everything."

She pouts and shoots me a playful look. "I'm at the *Metropolitan*. Under the name Veruca Salt. I'll be all alone tonight."

"Thanks again," I say and shut the door behind me.

The only person I want to be alone with is Laurent Grant, for whom I had a million questions.

CHAPTER EIGHT

LAURENT

That day in the ER parking lot, I learned some critical facts: it turned out that my dad wasn't only earning money from guiding fishing and diving tours. He was also doing some treasure hunting, searching for ships full of gold and silver that had been lost at sea.

It was a competitive, cutthroat world, especially when you're doing it without any government sanction or plans to report or cut them in on your findings.

Real modern-day pirate shit.

He and a rival group had stumbled upon a dive site that was loaded with doubloons, and each group claimed it for themselves.

When the rival group went out to dive one day, they found the great bulk of the treasure gone and went after my father for it. My mother knew a little bit about his "extracurricular" career, but not everything. I was blissfully unaware.

The guys who came to our house that day had already been to see my dad's business partner, Roger, earlier in the day, and they'd killed him when he refused to tell them anything.

My dad was the next target, but he was prepared for them and fought fire with fire.

When the feds came to investigate, they found a storage locker neither my mom nor I knew about that had millions of dollars in recovered treasure in it. They seized all of it. My mom got enough threatening phone calls that she feared for our future in Florida, and she uprooted us and took us to New Mexico, where we settled in Santa Fe.

We knew nobody in New Mexico. It was as if she picked it out of a hat. There was certainly no beach, and I was forbidden from joining the basketball team or doing much of anything else at my new school besides going to class and getting passing grades. I was expected to keep a low profile, like I was a ghost passing through the hallways. I doubt anybody from my graduating class remembers me. As the weird new kid senior year, I didn't make any friends.

The only good thing about New Mexico was our neighbor, Mrs. Rosales, an elderly grandmother who introduced me to New Mexico's chiles.

She was half-Mexican and half-Pueblo and grew up in a world filled with spices and flavors I'd never imagined. She taught me how to cook with Acoma, Zia, and Isleta chiles, as well as the more well-known green and red Hatch chiles.

I was drawn to her and her cooking, and despite never having had much interest in the kitchen prior to meeting her, it was like fate deposited us there, next door to her.

She was happy to teach, I was eager to learn (and to eat!), and before long, I developed an obsession with sauces and spices and creating my own.

I started researching culinary schools, as that made more sense to me than traditional college, but my mother saw the whole thing as a colossal waste of time. She wanted to go back to Jacksonville, convinced that there was more of Dad's treasure there somewhere, and that it was worth the risk to pursue it, along with her never-ending battle against the government to get what she considered her fair share of the seized assets (that would be all of it, according to Mom).

Shortly before I graduated high school, Mrs. Rosales's adult children had relocated her to Mexico to live with relatives, which made my decision to leave Santa Fe all

SEDUCED BY THE HOT CHEF | 59

the easier. The culinary scene in Las Vegas intrigued me, so I headed west. Mom returned to Jacksonville. I never saw her again.

I bounced around Las Vegas for a few years, getting in where I could, which proved difficult, as in Vegas who you know matters a great deal more than what you know.

Eventually, I hooked on at a barbecue place just off the Strip, *The Blue Rooster*, and things went well. I had an industrial kitchen in which to conduct my experiments, and I came up with some pretty popular rubs and sauces using a lot of what Mrs. Rosales taught me.

After a few years, the business began to thrive and started getting noticed by the local paper and then regional media dedicated to food and tourism. Big things seemed on the horizon for Laurent Grant and *The Blue Rooster*.

Until *he* showed up.

Trey Hale.

CHAPTER NINE

TREY

I somehow managed to graduate high school, even though I spent way more time on my bike than I did in a classroom.

My plan was to do whatever it took to get my Triple U patch, become a brother, and work my way up the ranks as quickly as possible. I knew most of the local and Vegas guys already, and my uncle Russell was well-connected.

What else could I want out of life?

"You're way better than all this," Russell told me one afternoon sitting on the back porch at the Triple U clubhouse in North Las Vegas.

"This is all I want," I shot back. "Besides, what's 'better' about me?"

"Well, even though you don't use them half the time, you've got brains. You can ride a hog anytime. But with this life... there's no pension. No retirement plans. I mean yeah, you set aside what you can and hope for the best, but you don't get insurance. Chances are, you wind up in the ground or locked up. That's it. My sister would have wanted more for you than riding into the cemetery or prison. Hell, kid, I want more for you than that.

I was an eighteen-year-old kid and feeling as cocky and indestructible as you'd expect. I argued and got pissed off at him for bringing up my mother, and the next thing you knew, I was on the ground fighting him.

Two brothers pulled us apart, and I wound up getting my ass kicked up one side of the clubhouse and down the other for daring to lift a finger against a patched-in Triple U, even if he was related to me.

Wayne, who wasn't yet president, told me that joining the MC at that point was a non-starter. He suggested I join the military, go away for a few years and come back with a new attitude and things might be different.

Enter Trey Hale, United States Marine.

Eight years later, finished with my four years in the reserves after four years active duty, my Harley and I were back in Las Vegas looking for purpose, direction, and a future.

A friend of Russell's was dating a waitress at a barbecue place just off the Strip, and they were looking to hire somebody as a catch-all – maintenance guy, dishwasher, bouncer for weekends when they had live bands perform.

As I was still working toward my Triple U patch and not earning yet, I took the job. Hard work for what didn't amount to a ton of money, but the position came with a perk beyond free (delicious) meals – Laurent Grant.

I can't completely explain what drew me to him, I mean besides a primal animal attraction to him that extended from his thick auburn mane to the tips of his toes and everywhere in-between.

But even my thick skull could tell that it was more than that. There was an energy to him that captured me and wouldn't let go. He had a confidence in him that was just sexy; the way he walked, the way he knew that not only was his food fantastic, but there was something inside him made of steel.

A tough yet elegant appeal that I found irresistible.

Like he'd been through the fire and come out not only unscathed but made stronger by it.

He was forged by heat.

Things never developed romantically like I hoped, but I never really pushed them too hard in that direction, either. I didn't want to risk the job, especially for the connection to my hopefully future Triple U MC brother, and more importantly I didn't want to do anything to push Laurent away.

At the time, it seemed like I had nothing but time.

A slow burn's not a bad thing, when you can feel the heat.

Eventually, I got my patch, and I really no longer needed the job, but as the saying goes, the heart wants what the heart wants (Okay, maybe there were other parts of me besides my *heart* that wanted things from Laurent, but I swear, my heart played a major role in all this!), so I stuck around a while to see how things would play out.

Becoming Laurent's boss was never part of the plan.

CHAPTER TEN

LAURENT

The first time I was introduced to Trey Hale, my heart just about stopped. He was a gorgeous hunk of ex-Marine with muscles in all the right places and eyes that, despite being ice blue, set my soul aflame.

Come on. Did I even really stand a chance?

Technically, I was his boss, but it was tough to give him direction when all I wanted was for him to grab me, push me up against the wall, and take me.

I'd never really understood that particular fantasy before; I was one who preferred my love sweet and sensual and slow. Trey awakened something wicked in me, and whenever we were together, I pictured those big rough hands of his, covered in grease from his motorcycle: all over me, holding me, restraining me, *spanking* me.

But I kept things professional.

Getting mixed up with coworkers is rarely a good idea, in my experience, even though in the restaurant business it seems like everybody is fucking everybody else.

At our restaurant, it turned out that the owner was fucking all of us.

As the business grew and more money started pouring in, rather than seeing improvements or getting raises, paychecks began bouncing from time to time and things like a busted urinal in the men's room started going weeks before being repaired. Vendors began demanding cash payments before they'd release bulk orders of things like napkins or food and we had to switch from Coke to Pepsi over unpaid invoices.

When the owner of a business is gambling away every penny he earns, that's the kind of shit that happens.

Things changed for a little while. The place got a badly needed facelift, a new sign and fresh coat of paint. We didn't need to race to the bank to cash our checks, and morale was boosted.

That lasted all of three weeks, until I checked my bank balance on a Monday morning to discover that my check had bounced again.

I called the owner and left an angry message but got no reply. When I showed up to work that afternoon, there was a sign on the door telling everybody to take the day off, but to come in the next day at the regular time.

And that we'd be paid for the day, which seemed miraculous.

When we arrived the next day, the sign out front, the one with the big blue chicken on it, was gone. As the staff slowly filtered in, we gave each other shrugs and shared whispers about what was happening. Once everybody had arrived, we looked at each other for direction.

That's when the new owner stood up and introduced himself.

"I think all of you know me, right? I'm Trey, Trey Hale. I'm the new owner of *Hale's Beef, Bikes, and Brews.*"

Shock and disbelief swirled through the room. I shifted my weight back and forth from foot to foot for a few minutes while the staff chattered among themselves before hearing Trey clear his throat to get their attention.

"As I said, I'm the new owner, we have a new name, but we're selling the same stuff as always – cold beer and the best barbecue in town. Right? What's in the past is in the past, I'm looking to the future. You're all getting paid for yesterday's day off. There won't be any more bounced paychecks and we're back in good standing with all our vendors," he said.

Calm, cool, and collected. The military precision contrasted with the wild biker's edge.

And now he owned the place?

Yeah, I never stood a chance.

CHAPTER ELEVEN

TREY

"How?" one of our line cooks asked. "Did you hit Megabucks or something?"

"Let's just say I have a wealthy... uncle. But make no mistake, I'm the boss, and this is a business. I'll make decisions accordingly. If anybody feels like they can't deal with the new arrangement, you're free to leave. But this place is going to be jumping in a couple hours, with plenty of money flowing. We have a band coming in tonight for the grand reopening, and I've got some hungry, *and thirsty*, friends coming, so let's do this."

The previous owner of *The Blue Rooster* had a serious gambling problem. When things got especially bad, he turned to the MC for a loan. When he lost that money as well, he satisfied the loan the only way he could – by signing the place over to the Triple U's.

Since I was already there and knew the business, I was installed as the boss and my name slapped on the place with only a tenuous connection to the MC.

Opening night was a smash success, with every Triple U on the west coast rolling in and filling the parking lot with choppers. We knew that wasn't healthy for the long-term success of the business, but for one night the place became our clubhouse. The waitresses never worked so hard, but nor did they ever go home with their pockets bulging quite so much.

More and more of my time was devoted to the restaurant, and before long we opened California locations and relocated the original store from just off-Strip to smack dab in the middle of Las Vegas Boulevard.

I missed the road, but I still got out to ride from time to time, mostly back and forth between *Hale's* shops. Our president, Wayne, shared my vision for long-term financial health for the club through the restaurants, but weaning some of the brothers off the drug teat would prove difficult.

That's where the Devil's Stepchildren stepped in, a black cloud with a silver lining that most of our guys, and all of theirs, lost the stomach for fighting once the bodies started piling up. Once I replaced President Wayne, virtually everyone came on board.

The night they fired their opening salvo had been a good one at *Hale's.* Laurent had taken a team from the restaurant across town to the *Sin City Blazin' Hot Chili Cookoff,* and he'd returned as a conquering hero, trophy in hand.

He and I celebrated with drinks and shut the place down together.

We sat in the office chatting, me telling Laurent how proud I was of him. It was late by the time we laughed our way together out into the parking lot, and as we walked, our hands bumped against each other a couple times. Without thinking, I threw an arm around his shoulders and pulled him tight to my chest.

I released him, but somehow our fingers wound up intertwined. I turned to face him, and he looked up at me with this smile, the faint glow of neon illuminating his face.

Cheesy as hell? You bet.

But the moment was what the moment was, and it had been one of the best in my life.

I smiled back at him and our eyes locked together. Years of trying to ignore my attraction to him dissolved. My hand moved up to his face, cradling his cheeks. Then it happened. I leaned down and kissed him, tentatively at first, but the way he responded made me want to *devour* him.

I kissed Laurent back harder, and his mouth encouraged me, so I continued. He kissed me deeply, and our hands started exploring. I found the ass I'd admired for so long and cupped it, pulling him tight against me, where I was sure he could feel the effect he'd had on me. He was too short for me to tell if I was having the same effect on him.

I was just about to suggest taking things elsewhere, someplace a little more private, when my phone rang. Wayne's ring tone. Had to answer.

And everything changed in an instant.

CHAPTER TWELVE

LAURENT

Trey Hale was going to be my *boss*? Holy new power dynamic making me want him even more, Batman!

We all knew the MC was the money and the power behind Trey, but after that first night we rarely saw many brothers from the club around.

Too many bikes and bikers wouldn't be good for business.

Eventually, things went so well that we moved to a location on the Strip, a bigger, fancier place that managed to retain the spirit of the original.

I was making more money than ever before and starting to dream of maybe bottling some of my sauces and selling them beyond the *Hale's* web site.

I traveled to each of our new locations to train the staff and teach them how to properly cook our signature dishes. Trey and I had a great working relationship, more partners than boss and subordinate. In many ways I was his right-hand... err, *man*, and the *Hale's* chain grew and thrived.

Trey suggested that I enter the annual *Sin City Blazin' Hot Chili Cookoff* under the *Hale's* banner. We didn't normally serve chili, but he knew I could pull it off.

After six weeks of experimenting with different recipes and combinations and having my New Mexico chile people hook me up with the best fresh ingredients they could find, I hit pay dirt. It was Texas-style chili with New Mexico influences and my own secret twist.

It killed.

No, not in the motorcycle club sense, in the sense that it kicked ass. It won the biggest trophy and the culinary media raved about me as a "rising star."

When I walked through the front door of *Hale's* holding that trophy, Trey had the biggest smile I'd ever seen grace his rugged face.

He picked me up and swung me around, lifting me as effortlessly as if I were one of the boxes of our paper to-go cups from the storeroom. It was the first time I felt his hands on me like that, demonstrating that his muscles were for more than just show.

We shut the place down that night, drinking probably a little more than was safe for me to drive, and seeing off the entire staff until it was just he and I in the office.

I didn't know if he shared even a smidgen of my attraction to him, and I knew that he was bi but mostly hooked up with women, but I would have been perfectly fine with him sweeping the papers off his desk and having me right there.

Instead, he suggested that it had been a long day, and that I must be tired, and that he'd walk me to my car.

That's when he stood up and twisted to grab his helmet and his dick pulsed in his pants at me. His thick slab of manhood, right there where I could reach out and grab it.

Or taste it.

Oh lord.

As we walked, we were shoulder to shoulder, our hands brushing together in a way that made me wish he'd just grab mine and hold it. He didn't of course, and we stepped out into a cooling evening and he threw an arm around me in kind of a drunk frat brother way.

"I'm so proud of you, Laurent," he said, his deep voice with those rough edges that sent tingles down my spine every time he spoke. "This whole thing only works because of you. You're amazing."

He turned to face me, and I looked up into his eyes expectantly. I knew it was impossible, but I could hope, right?

Except it wasn't impossible.

Trey Hale bent down and kissed me. A peck at first, but my body wasn't about to be satisfied with that.

I kissed him back, his hand on my face and my arms wrapped 'round his neck, pulling him in. The kiss was fucking fantastic, the perfect blend of lips and tongue and pressure and everything. I breathed him in and he me and we melted together.

He reached down and took a handful of my ass and I yelped into his mouth as he pulled me tight against him. His erection was muscular and throbbing as it nestled between us, and I felt myself getting hard in anticipation and response. And I wanted more. I wanted to be filled by him.

But then his phone rang. And you know the rest.

It was like history repeating itself in a way. A man I... well, I can't say I *loved* Trey Hale then, but he was pretty damn near and dear to me.

Give it a minute and I have no doubt I would have fallen so hard for him, there would have been no road back.

So, another man who meant the world to me had my world exploding in violence, even though I'd done nothing to deserve it or invite it except exist.

Once I was free, after Tick intervened, I knew I had to leave, had to disappear, had to put Trey out of mind and out of my life forever. I decided that on my frantic drive to Tanya's house, that I'd never place myself in the line of fire again.

Of course, I couldn't stave off every act of random violence in the world, nobody can do that, but I could remove myself from places and people who'd proven themselves to be dangerous.

People like Trey Hale.

Except here I am, preparing to return to Las Vegas. And not only that, to return to *Hale's Beef, Bikes, and Brews*, site of the chili cookoff.

When I entered the contest, they hadn't yet announced where it would take place. Had I known I never would have entered. I'd have found another way to keep *Uncle Waylon's* fresh and relevant and get my product on television beyond just the late-night television commercials and social media advertising we are doing.

The FBI assure me that the Devil's Stepchildren are no longer a threat.

I am less worried about them than coming face-to-face with Trey Hale, especially considering the fact that I totally ghosted him, and he has no idea I am coming. The name "Will Laughlin" wouldn't mean anything to him.

Not that I kid myself he's been waiting around pining after me.

But we'd been friends and colleagues at least, and I know there'll be a reckoning for the way things ended.

Of that I'm sure.

Of other things? Less so.

How would I react when I walked into *Hale's* to inevitably find him with his arm around some 22-year-old model?

A guy like Trey Hale does not stay single. He is too much man to do without getting that big hog of his regularly serviced, of that I have no doubt. The fact that it would never be me on the receiving end of his sexual fury saddens me, but I can console myself with that trophy, all that free publicity, and raking in all the money that will hopefully follow.

Eye on the prize, boy. Eye on the prize.

Pride to the side.

CHAPTER THIRTEEN

TREY

The *Eat This!* team arrives two days before the contest kicking off to get their equipment in place and squash any last-minute bugs. The judges have a meeting at *Hale's* over dinner that same night. Two celebrity chefs with cooking shows on *Eat This!* network, a former mayor of Las Vegas, the reigning Miss USA from chili world capital Texas, and a recently retired NFL quarterback with two Super Bowl rings round out the jury.

Not a bad lineup, I guess.

I'd have been happy with them eating anywhere else. All that needs to happen is for one of them to have a dish they don't like, or to coincidentally get sick the next day, and all of a sudden, we have no shot at defending our trophy.

Sure, the tastings are all supposed to be blind, but there are always rumors that judges got info leaked to them and make decisions accordingly.

And human beings are unpredictable under the best of circumstances.

With two Texans on the docket, the beauty queen and the quarterback, all that probably has to happen is for one of them to decide that *Hale's* stuff isn't from Texas and we'll be out of the running. The chili world is very provincial.

I watch the judges file in. I've met the two chefs and our former mayor before, of course, but the other two are new to me.

The Miss USA is so skinny I wonder if she ever ate much of anything, but she is apparently one of those *"I eat cheeseburgers and fries and milkshakes all the time and I never work out, but I'm a size zero!"* girls all women love so much, so maybe she can put away some chili when called upon.

The quarterback seems like a nice guy, but he'd cost me a bundle of money by winning that second Super Bowl, so I am cordial but not overly friendly.

Very professional and mature of me, I know. It was totally his fault I lost all that money, right?

I stick around for a little while until they are served, but it is too stressful, the chance of a mishap too present, and I excuse myself.

Better not to make it look like I'm trying to influence or buddy up with the judges either, come to think of it.

The Strip is packed, so I take a back road away from it and pick up Las Vegas Boulevard farther south, past Mandalay Bay. I switch over to the interstate and roll out to Stateline and beyond. I get up over 100 MPH, half-hoping some California highway patrolman takes the bait and I can lose him in the desert, but nothing doing.

I stop in Baker at the *Mad Greek* for the world's best strawberry milkshake before heading back to Vegas. I get a text from my main man back at *Hale's* with a string of thumbs-up emojis to let me know the meal has gone well. I release a big breath and tug my helmet back on.

Less than forty-eight hours remain until I lock eyes with Laurent Grant again.

At this rate, I'm counting every damn second.

CHAPTER FOURTEEN

LAURENT

The lights of Las Vegas come into view, mostly the same as I remember, but with subtle differences. Las Vegas is an ever-changing, constantly evolving organism.

New hotel towers had sprung up to replace some of the ones I'd been familiar with, and others have new signs or color schemes. I travel with two assistants, have suites booked at *the Venetian*, and kitchen space and time reserved at a local caterer so I can prepare everything perfectly.

I'll see Trey, sure, but it will be ancillary to my main purpose of winning. We are adults, we can leave the past where it was. No problem.

A town car takes us to our hotel, and I make sure my helpers are settled in before I go down to the casino. The old, familiar Las Vegas energy is all around me, cash flying, hopes and dreams being shattered in one corner of the casino while new millionaires are being minted in another.

I long to walk the Strip, so I find the front entrance and step out into the neon madness.

Part of me has missed this in a way that I can't totally even verbalize.

For my two assistants, Beth and Trev, it is a first visit to Las Vegas. I told them to take the night off, go out and have fun, but to be ready to work the next day, so not to overdo it. They'll have the opportunity to party as hard as they can handle, on my dime, once we've won the top prize at the cookoff.

I start walking down the Strip, gazing up at the spectacle. There are throngs of people everywhere; an entire wedding party, screaming, laughing and celebrating. Guys slapping brochures against their hands advertising "Girls! Direct to your room!" Pale middle-aged Midwesterners looking confused. Guys in their twenties thinking they are much cooler than they actually are.

I slip into one of the biggest casinos and play a few spins on my favorite game, roulette. I hit a few split numbers and quickly run my initial $200 up to over

$500. The gambling gods are smiling on me. Hopefully the culinary gods feel the same way.

As I leave the cashier's cage and head back toward the street, I am stopped by a pair of women who look to be in their mid-70's, maybe older.

"Oh my god, you were on the TV!" one of them exclaims.

Her friend cocks her head and looks me up and down as if giving me an appraisal. "Right! *The Abby and Brian Show!* You're that singer!"

I smile awkwardly. "No, sorry, I can't sing. Not me," I say and try to move past them.

"No, Margaret," the first woman scolds her friend. "That's not him. He was on *Joe with the Joes*. It's my favorite show." She turns toward me. "You're that boy with the sauces."

My eyes flick from side to side, hopeful that nobody will overhear or notice me. I nod. "That's right."

"I knew it!" the first woman replies, smacking a hand against her thigh. "Mitchell isn't going to believe this. Neither are the ladies at bridge. Oh my god. Oh my god. I knew we'd meet somebody famous in Las Vegas!"

Her friend looks like she might faint. I wonder how they'd react if they bumped into an actual celebrity. And then it suddenly occurred to me that, yeah, I have been on *national* television.

National meant that it aired everywhere in the nation, which includes Las Vegas. While I don't exactly expect Trey Hale to be a fan of *Joe with the Joes*, there may be every chance the grapevine found its way to him and he might know I am here.

Four years of nerves and second-guessing myself and building up the courage to return to Las Vegas all hit me at once and I feel tears welling up in my eyes.

"I'm sorry," I say to the women and brush past a group of people standing near the doorway involved in some sort of heated argument, and I am once again back outside.

I take deep breaths and put my head down. I just need to get back to my room and take an Ambien and get a good night's sleep. I'll wake up in the morning and have a good breakfast, take Trev and Beth out to one of my favorite spots in Las Vegas, Red Rock Canyon, then we'll come back and spend the late afternoon and evening preparing our food.

Everything would be fine.

Better than fine.

It will be great. I can do this.

I walk briskly, purposefully, my head down, getting myself focused. I am fine. Everything is going to be good. I'd built *Uncle Waylon's* into a success, I am living my dream, the past would stay right where it –

My thoughts are interrupted by the unmistakable roar of a Harley. No, two Harleys. They pull out of the driveway just ahead of me, a pair of hogs, ridden by men dressed in leather. Familiar leather. As they turn and head north on Las Vegas Boulevard, I see their backs – Triple U MC Las Vegas Chapter.

I stop in my tracks and look up. I am standing right in front of *Hale's Beef, Bikes, and Brews.*

When I left the casino, I was flustered. I got turned around and went right instead of left, and here I am. I take a deep breath and stand stone still as waves of people move past me in both directions.

That's when I see him.

Trey Hale.

CHAPTER FIFTEEN

TREY

The ride out to Baker and the milkshake are just appetizers for the main course; the good news about the meal the judges ate at *Hale's*.

On the ride back, in light traffic, I get my hog up over 130 MPH approaching Stateline. I envy the old-timers who could do it without a helmet. At that speed, helmet or no, if I crash it is all over, but I still comply with the helmet law, even as I ignore the speed limit completely.

I make the return trip to *Hale's* in record time, covering the hundred miles between Baker, California, and Vegas in just a hair over fifty-five minutes.

It takes another fifteen to get from my exit off the interstate to the parking lot. I park and touch base with a couple of MC brothers in from L.A. who'd just finished dinner before heading out to hit the tables.

People find it odd that I do things like pick up trash in the parking lot, seeing as I'm the owner of *Hale's* and the president of the Tripe U MC, but it's that ownership and leadership position that make me want to set the example, to help instill pride in my staff and my club.

So, yeah, I empty trash cans, wash the occasional window, and do whatever needs to be done.

Except scrub toilets.

I have to draw the line somewhere.

That's what well paid pledges are for.

Anyway, on Las Vegas Boulevard open container laws are largely ignored, so beer bottles wind up *everywhere*. An especially popular spot is on the waist-high base of the streetlight at the edge of our driveway. It is completely filled with cups and bottles, which just looks trashy, so I grab a trash bag from inside and walk out toward the Strip to clean up the mess.

As I approach, I shake the bag open with a loud *snap*, which startles some of the tourists. I don't mind that, since so many of them are completely oblivious to their surroundings as they walk with either their jaws hanging open and heads tilted back taking in the architecture or face down looking at their phones.

Snapping them out of their distracted states, even for a moment, is my version of community service.

You're in Vegas.

Actually experience it.

I am nearly to the light to grab the bottles when I stop dead in my tracks.

A group of college kids make me lose sight of him for a moment, but when they pass, our eyes meet and it's like I've been hit by a freight train. My pulse hammers and my vision narrows down to one single point in the universe.

Laurent Grant is standing ten feet away from me.

CHAPTER SIXTEEN

LAURENT

My heart thumps against my rib cage like an angry beast trying to break out of a cage and I suddenly can't breathe.

Trey is standing right there, almost close enough to touch.

My mouth moves, but words don't come. His hand covers his mouth, then he pulls his fingers together and tugs at his bottom lip. It is something he does when he is nervous.

Something adorable and sexy all at once.

He is dressed all in black, from his boots to the leather that covers the rest of him. He has on his club vest, with the word "President" emblazoned across the left side of his chest.

Trey is the president of the Triple U MC?

Things really have changed while I've been away.

A rowdy group of fraternity douchebags approaches from the right, which necessitated me moving, either closer to Trey or backwards, into the street.

I step forward tentatively and barely miss being stampeded right off the sidewalk.

"Settle the fuck down," Trey growls, stepping forward and to the side to confront the group. "And apologize."

"Or what?" a heavyset guy in a blue suit, rainbow clown wig, and sunglasses replies. He was the largest member of the group, but several of them looked large and sturdy. They form a semicircle around Trey, who takes a step toward the clown with a grin on his face.

"Or I'll make you eat that wig and those sunglasses. And wash them down with all your teeth. How's that sound?"

The guy removes his sunglasses and squints hard at Trey, who leans in until the tips of their noses almost touch.

"There's five of us and one you, dude. Step off before you get beat down," one of the group threatens, raising a hand and pushing Trey's shoulder. Trey didn't budge, staring into the clown's eyes with a ferocity that holds my complete attention.

His full-on protector mode is........very hot.

"Sorry. We're sorry," the clown says, easing back away from Trey and turning toward me. "Are you okay?"

I nodded.

"We don't want any trouble, man," the guy in the clown wig says, offering his hand to Trey.

The guy who had previously threatened Trey pipes up. "Didn't think you were such a little *bitch*, Murph. Can't believe you backed down from him."

"Shut the fuck up, Alex," the clown-wigged guy mutters to his friend. Then he leans in closer and half-whispers, "He's a biker, dude. Like in a legit gang. See his patch? Fuck that."

"Have a good night. Stay out of trouble," Trey says, shaking the guy's hand. When he breaks the grip, the guy in the clown wig grimaces and rubs his hand. The group ambles away, arguing among themselves.

Trey turned toward me and gives me a slow, easy smile.

"It's been a while," he says, his voice even deeper than it was when he was confronting the men.

"Yeah," is all I could muster. I look down at the ground and kick a pebble. Suddenly, I can't bear to meet his gaze. It is too intense and there's a wash of emotion that hits me so hard that even though I'm braced for it, it threatens to sweep me away.

"Should I call you Laurent or Will?"

"Laurent," I say quietly. "Trey, I'm sorry."

"Hmm," he grunts, considering my apology. "So am I."

"You're president of the MC now?"

He looks down at his chest. "That's what the patch says. But these days I feel more like a restaurant owner than anything else."

"Restaurant *mogul*," I correct, looking up at him almost shyly. "Seems like you're doing really well."

"Yeah, *Hale's* is going gangbusters. No doubt. We're opening our first Arizona location next month."

"Congrats," I say, really meaning it.

Christ, this is awkward. There's so much to say and yet, even though I've imagined this conversation a thousand times, I can't seem to bring myself to actually say the right words.

And fear clenches at me, like this opportunity – this chance to be near this man I've spent so much time thinking about – might fade away.

Slip right through my fingers, like so many other things over the years.

"Want to go somewhere we can talk?" he asks. The hustle and bustle of the Strip isn't exactly conducive to conversation.

"I'd like that."

"I think I can rustle up a helmet inside if you want to ride along with me."

"Is that okay?" I ask. I have on jeans, Oxfords, and a light sweater. Not exactly motorcycle chic, but I figure I'll be safe if we aren't going far.

"What do you mean?" he asks, his eyebrows bunching in apparent confusion at my question.

"I meant like I didn't want to cause any trouble with your gang or whatever, that's all. I understand if this is weird or inconvenient; I didn't mean for, you know, this to go down like *this*," I stammer. My cheeks flame bright red and if I could wish myself anywhere else in the universe right now I would.

I'm completely mortified.

But he's looking at me, something softening the lines of his ruggedly handsome face and a certain sparkle in his eyes that has me licking my lips.

Trey chuckles softly.

"Who I ride with is no one's business but mine," he says, not breaking eye contact. "You're the last person I kissed."

He turns and walks toward *Hale's*, leaving me stunned.

CHAPTER SEVENTEEN

TREY

I go inside my place and rummage up a spare helmet from my office. It isn't much to look at, but it looks like it would fit. I pop into the bathroom to look at myself in the mirror.

Laurent Grant.

Alive and well, in my parking lot, and ready to climb on the back of my bike.

Just when you think you have life figured out…

He looks *good*. Damn good. He's put on a little weight since last I saw him, but in all the right places. Filled out, you could say, though he still looks as classy and elegant as ever. He has a glow about him. Success looks fantastic on him.

I splash a little water from the sink on my face, check my teeth in the mirror, and head back outside to find him standing next to my bike.

"This is the only one in the lot that looked like a president's bike," Laurent said with a smile.

His smile makes me weak and hard all at the same time.

It is late, so I take us to somewhere I know would be open, but quiet – *Pancake Jack's*, a twenty-four-hour breakfast place on the east side of town.

I drive slowly and carefully in deference to Laurent, and he clutches at me from behind. It is a few blocks away, and as I guessed, mostly empty. The feel of his body molded against mine, the heat is almost enough to make me keep driving.

Keep driving out to some amazing secluded spot so we can be totally alone.

But I remind myself that's not what this is.

We're just here to talk.

Regardless of whatever signals my cock is trying to throw out,

We get a booth in the far corner, away from the half dozen customers scattered on the other side.

"Don't know if ghosts get hungry, but this place makes mean Belgian waffles," I say. I eat at *Jack's* at least once or twice a week when I am in town. It is comfort food at its finest.

"I'm no ghost," he counters. "But sure, I think a waffle sounds good."

We order and sit quietly as the server brings over our drinks. Neither of us really knows how to start, so I drain my orange juice and put both palms flat on the table. I lean back and take a long, appreciative look at Laurent.

Damn, he is a handsome man.

"You say you aren't a ghost, but you flat-out disappeared, Laurent. Dropped off the face of the earth. Nobody knew anything. Even if you were just an employee of mine, that would be upsetting. But you were more than that. Much more.

"And I was left with nothing. Well, not nothing, I was left with four dead bodies and you missing. I didn't know if you were being held hostage somewhere or dead, or..."

He raises a hand to cut me off.

"Trey," Laurent begins then gets quiet and looks close to tears. Seeing that look on his face makes me want to kill something, hurt whatever's causing him pain.

But instead, I reach across the table and take his hands in mine.

"Whatever it is, just know, end of the day, I'm thrilled that you're okay... Or at least that you seem to be okay. And I'm pretty sure I can move beyond whatever it is. I've missed you, Bear. I really have. I spent a lot of sleepless nights and expended a lot of resources, club and personal, looking for you.

"But I have to say, you look great, and I saw your piece on TV and I was pretty blown away by what you've built. I do have some questions about the whole *Trey's Big Hog* thing, though," I give him my best grin, trying not to look too hopeful.

That gets him laughing, then he swiftly wipes a tear from his eye, but it is more just a release of nerves and relief than from any kind of sadness.

Our food arrives, and we cut into our waffles and eat some bacon quietly before he is ready to try again.

"I never told you about my father," Laurent says, and I shake my head no, even as I try to recalibrate my thoughts and figure out where this is going.

"Okay. Whew." He wipes a tear from his cheek and begins a story about a life in Florida I knew nothing about. It culminates with his father's murder basically in front of him and how he fled with his mother to New Mexico.

I am flabbergasted.

Laurent was a clean cut kind of guy, but he always had a certain toughness, a quiet steel that came from somewhere I could never pinpoint. Now I knew. A trauma like that either leaves you crippled or galvanizes you. He found strength in it, because of course he did.

He is Laurent fucking Grant.

CHAPTER EIGHTEEN

LAURENT

I finish telling Trey a story I'd never told a single soul in the fifteen years since it happened.

Not even my closest friends in Las Vegas know about my father. And once I became Will Laughlin, Laurent Grant ceased to exist. When it has ever come up, I have a well-rehearsed story about my folks getting killed in a car accident in Virginia.

The emotional weight I haven't even realized I carry dissipates, and I exhale and shake out my limbs. Trey has been holding my hands atop the table since I began, and I don't want him to *ever* let go, but the pent-up energy has to be released.

Plus his huge hands engulf mine, and he's got a strength that's staggering.

"I don't have any idea what to say," Trey replies. "Except that it really sucked what happened to your dad. To your parents. If I thought there was anybody to go after, I'd have a whole fleet of my brothers on the road to Jacksonville first thing tomorrow morning to get you some justice."

"I know," I answer. "And I'm grateful. But it was so long ago. And it would only open up old wounds."

Trey nods. "Still…"

"But that's why, and I hope you understand, when we… that night, I was jumped. Three of those guys…"

"Devil's Stepchildren," Trey completes my thought. "They've been… *eliminated.* Erased."

"I'm sorry about your friend. He saved me."

"Tick? Yeah, that was a tough one. Of everybody we've lost, he was the toughest one to swallow, I think. He and Wayne, he was the president of the club before me. Tell me what happened that night?" Trey asks. "If you can. If you can't, I get it. No pressure."

I tell him about the guys grabbing me, kicking the guy in the balls, and then Tick showing up. As I get to the part about him taking on all three of them, allowing me to escape, Trey's eyes glaze over and redden. His cheeks flushed with emotion and he put his face in his hands.

That show of vulnerability takes me by surprise, and has a certain warmth rising in my chest.

I have to glance away, because my own eyes are getting misty.

"I wish there were a hundred more of those assholes around, so I could take them out, one by one," he says, his voice rough with emotion. "For Tick. And for you. I'm so sorry, Bear. I don't blame you for running and not looking back. I should never have pressured you for a kiss. For anything. You're in a different class. A rising star like you doesn't belong with trash like us."

Every word hits me like a kick to the gut.

I have to let him know that he's wrong. That he's a good person, and that he never, ever pressured me.

I get up and move over to his side of the booth. He scoots in to make room for me. I want to hug him. I'd never seen such an emotional side of gruff, no-nonsense Trey Hale.

Part of me, as ridiculous as this sounds, wants to protect his heart from this tough, hard world.

A marine and a biker doesn't need my protection, I know.

And yet.

I put my arms around his shoulders, and he put his around my waist, such as he could in the cramped confines of the booth.

"Trey," I say, keeping my voice very soft. "I'd been *dying* for you to kiss me since the first time I ever saw you. Since the day you walked into *the Blue Rooster*. I haven't kissed anybody since that night, either."

Trey leans back and looks me in the eye, our arms still tangled up with one another.

"As handsome as you are?" Trey says his voice almost a growl. "Guys must be lined up from Knoxville to Toronto for a crack at you."

"And you expect me to believe the president of the Triple U Motorcycle Club doesn't have every stripper, croupier, and biker in Las Vegas beating a path to your bedroom door?"

"I never said I didn't have plenty of options," he says with a laugh. "And opportunities. I just said I hadn't pursued any of them. Too busy chasing a ghost."

"Well, you caught him," I say with delight. My smile is one of those ones that are so big they hurt. I hope I didn't look too ridiculous.

"Yes, I did," he replies. He pulls his phone out of his pocket, makes a show of powering it down, then shoves it back in his pocket.

Then he leans in to kiss me. Again.

CHAPTER NINETEEN

TREY

I kiss Laurent because I *have* to. I can't stand being in his presence for another breath, another heartbeat, without tasting that perfect mouth of his again.

Kissing somebody in a diner booth, all twisted sideways, isn't ideal. But I'd have kissed him underwater, in a mine shaft, upside down, anywhere I got the chance.

I've had a Laurent-sized hole in my heart for too long.

We make out like teenagers, ignoring the waitress who left a check and the busboy who cleared our table. I kiss his mouth, his throat, his cheeks and forehead, everywhere I can get to.

After a while, as our hands explore where they can, given the circumstances, it becomes clear we need to get somewhere private.

Immediately.

"Laurent," I say, pulling just far enough away to get him focused on what is coming out of my mouth rather than where else I could put it on his face and neck. "I don't want to come across as too forward, but…"

"But if we don't get out of here right now, I'm going to get arrested for tearing all your clothes off, followed by mine," he says breathlessly.

I wiped the saliva from my bottom lip and smile. "My place isn't far from here."

"Yes, please," he says with a grin.

I throw a hundred-dollar bill on the table and we head for my hog. I don't drive nearly as slowly or cautiously to my house as I had from the Strip to *Pancake Jack's*. I say a silent prayer of thanks that my cleaning lady had been by earlier that same day.

I haven't been home since, but she always did a great job so I know Laurent will be getting the best possible impression of how I lived.

My house is Old Vegas, built in the 60s by a mobster. It has a sunken living room and some oddball architecture, but it works for me. The hot tub and pool out back are terrific perks, especially for a kid from

Tonopah who used to sneak into the tiny pools at the run-down hotels we had in Tonopah at night, once they closed, to get relief from the desert heat.

I lead Laurent inside, and once I lock the front door, we are back at it. I push him up against the wall next to the door and take his wrists, pulling them up above his head and pinning them there and kissing him aggressively.

"Are you sure you want this, Laurent? You have to tell me. You don't understand how bad I want you. How much I've thought about this moment. I won't be able to stop once I start. I want you so fucking bad, boy."

He stares back into my eyes defiantly. "Do it. Use me every way you know how. I want you so much."

CHAPTER TWENTY

LAURENT

I can't believe what I am saying.

It isn't me at all, but on the other hand, it is the first time I've been authentically *me* in years. There is no more Will Laughlin, no more *Uncle Waylon's,* no more fear, no more running and hiding. All that is left is me and Trey.

Our desire. Our passion. Our *need.*

He tugs at my sweater, pulling it up and over my head. Once it reaches my wrists, instead of pulling it off, he twists the arms around my wrists and ties them tightly, restraining them. I whimper with surprise. My entire body feels like it is aflame and crackling. I kick off my shoes as he sets his sights on my button up shirt.

"Sorry. I'll buy you another one," Trey growls in a low voice, and I don't know what he means until he rips it open and one button after another pops off and falls to the floor.

Holy shit, this is so hot.

He turns me back around, hands still over my head, and he puts a finger beneath my chin. "My eyes. Look into my eyes."

I nod and lock my gaze on his.

"Nowhere but right here," he says pointing to his incandescently blue eyes.

Like I could ever want to look at anything – in this moment or ever again, maybe. It feels like I could stare into those eyes forever.

I repeat my nod. Every nerve ending on my body is on full alert, and it seems like the thermostat in his house must be set for two hundred degrees.

He drags the back of his hand across my hardened nipples and I nearly faint.

My knees buckle, and I squirm and mew as he does it again and again.

"You're so hot, Bear," he says, and kisses me.

I let my arms fall over his head and let my bound wrists rest on the back of his neck as we kiss.

He reaches down and undoes my jeans, pushing them and my briefs down around my hips and to my ankles, where I kick them away.

His lips command mine, as his hand finds my throbbing sex and he brushes his thumb over my head, gently caressing me there. I pull him as tight against me as I am able as he becomes more and more aggressive with his fingers.

They wrap their way around my member and I'm completely at his mercy.

"I've thought of making you come for so long, Laurent. Will you come for me?" he growls into my ear as his powerful, grease stained hand strokes me up and down.

Everything tenses at once when he touches it, and when his mouth meets mine again, I kiss him desperately. I stand up on my tiptoes, that magic spot inside me so sensitive it frightens me. There is no escape from the onrushing wave, however. He just keeps massaging me *there*, and when his thumb slips over my head, I cry out as a cataclysmic orgasm overwhelms me.

All the way through the sexual maelstrom that rages through me, I clutch at him to somehow keep my soul from shattering into a million pieces and dissolving into infinity.

I scream into his mouth again and again as wave after wave buffets me before mercifully setting me on a cloud made of pure bliss.

As my knees finally give out completely, he scoops me up and carries me into his bedroom. I am only vaguely aware of my surroundings. All I know is ecstasy, and it's all I crave, more than oxygen, water, or countless other irrelevant things.

He lays me on the bed and undoes the sweater on my wrists, freeing me.

I writhe on the bed, reveling in my nakedness. If I never wear clothes again, so be it.

If I never leave Trey Hale's bed again, all the better.

CHAPTER TWENTY-ONE

TREY

Laurent's orgasm was glorious. It just kept going and going and every time he screamed or moaned it made my cock progressively harder.

It got to the point that I thought I might not be able to wait.

And there's no way I'm rushing this, or not making the most of this most wonderous opportunity that I have been given.

I still can't believe this perfect specimen of man is in my bed.

As he lays on my bed, I slowly remove my vest, black shirt, boots, and pants. All that remain are my boxer briefs.

"Oh my god," he gasps as I stand up straight after pulling my pants all the way off. "I need that so fucking bad, Trey. Please don't make me wait any longer." He points to the obscene bulge stretching my underwear.

I grin and climb onto the bed, leaving them on for the time being. I get between Laurent's legs and begin kissing him again, pressing down with my hardness between his legs. I can feel the heat rising from him through the material.

As I press down, I rotate my hips slowly as I kiss him.

Laurent moans and his eyes roll back as he bucks his hips toward me. As the desire takes hold of him, I bend my mouth down to his chest, sucking his nipples forcefully. He makes sounds from deep in his throat as I continue grinding and sucking.

Just as it starts to look like he can't take anymore, I reached down, pulled my briefs down far enough to release my cock, and press my head against his asshole.

He goes rigid and he claws at my shoulders and upper back, gritting his teeth.

"Do you have protection…" he asks as I push against him, feeling his warm, soft skin already relaxing to welcome my cock and thinking that I understand what it's like to be in heaven.

"Please!" he begs. The classy, elegant Laurent Grant I'd fallen for revealed a side of himself I never knew existed. I'm not sure he knew it existed.

And I love it.

I rush to slip on a rubber and lube up before I fuck him as hard as I am able, my hands sliding down under his ass to pull him against me even as I thrust deeper.

Deeper and harder.

Claiming.

Mine.

Never letting go.

"Never... stop... fucking... me!" he implores as a litany of curse words tumbled out of his sexy mouth.

The way he responds to everything I do to him, the way he keeps getting hard again after coming, intensely kissing me and pulling me in tighter with his legs and arms, makes it impossible for me to continue without my own release.

"Laurent... I can't... You just feel so good I can't hold it much longer..."

CHAPTER TWENTY-TWO

LAURENT

"I need it so bad, Trey," I beg, the shock at my own delicious wantonness somewhere just beyond the edges of my awareness. "Come. Use my body to come. I've wanted your come for so long. I'll do anything to make you come."

He reaches down and places one of his large hands around my throat.

Not squeezing, just making sure I remain exactly where I am, right where he and his amazing dick need me to be.

He jackhammers into me, fifteen, then twenty violent thrusts, then he roars like he was in agony, but I could feel that what he is experiencing was anything but pain. With each thrust and throb, I feel him emptying himself into me. My body responds in kind, climaxing again, this time from my prostrate, one that made me tremble all over.

He kisses me softly as the last few tremors course through our bodies, and he slides to the side of me, his arm remaining draped across my chest.

He cups my shoulder with his hand and pulls me to my side, where we kiss, and he runs his fingertips up and down my side and back.

"Laurent, I love you," he says, sounding both confident and vulnerable in a way that leaves me breathless. "I have for years. For so long. I've never deserved you. I still don't. You're the most incredible, brilliant man I've ever met. I don't know what you're doing with me, but I love you so much."

I wipe tears from my eyes and bury my face in his shoulder as he held me.

"I'm so sorry I left you," I whisper into the crook of his neck. "I missed you every single day. There's no one like you. I've never wanted anyone else. I never will."

After we rest a while, we resume with slow, passionate love. Long, deep thrusts into my soul. He fills me again, marking me as his. No man could make my body experience the things Trey Hale can.

I wouldn't want to let them try.

We fall asleep all tangled up with each other, a deep, dreamless sleep. It is the first time I'd felt safe in many, many years.

I know Trey Hale could and would give his life to protect me if need be.

I never want to sleep anywhere ever again but in his arms.

CHAPTER TWENTY-THREE

TREY

When we wake up the next morning, it is barely still morning, and our phones are both filled with missed calls and texts.

"Will's" two assistants have been frantically trying to locate their missing boss and my brothers are concerned that something may have happened to their president. Two of my lieutenants came by my house and claimed to have pounded on the front door, but we were too far gone to hear them, or care if we had.

I am the first to stir, and I find Laurent's head still nestled against my chest as sunlight streams in through cracks in the blinds, giving him a soft glow, making him look like a fallen angel.

God, he is beautiful. I brush a few stray strands away from his face and kiss his forehead. I need to get up to use the bathroom, but my arm is pinned beneath his neck. I slip away as quietly as I can, but when I return, I find him propped up on her elbows in the bed, smiling. The sheet doesn't quite reach his freckled chest.

I stop to admire the view, and he sticks his tongue out at me.

"You let me sleep way too long, mister. I think this whole thing was strategy on your part, so I wouldn't have time to cook."

"Here I thought I was supposed to be the notorious criminal, but you're the one with the devious mind," I say, sliding back into bed next to him.

"But if it's a choice," I continued, leaning down to cover his collarbone with kisses, "between staying in bed with you," my mouth reached his chest, kissing shrinking concentric circles around his nipples, "and cooking chili for some contest, well, chili is gonna lose." I capture his left nipple in my teeth and he sharply sucks in a breath. "Every damn time."

One thing leads to another, and an hour later, having explored his body with tongue, hands, and cock, we finally make our way to the shower and reluctantly back out into the real world.

After one amazing final go in the shower, with Laurent pressed up against the glass of my shower as I thrust deep inside him from behind.

There's nothing this man can't make amazing.

The next day, under the hot lights of the *Eat This!* production team, the annual *Sin City Blazin' Hot Chili Cookoff* takes place.

Stacia Salt shows up as flirty as ever, but between the glare Laurent gives her and the way Laurent and I keep kissing, I think she got the message that I was off-limits.

Despite being the host, and two-time defending champion, the entry representing *Hale's* not only didn't win the grand prize, it didn't finish in the top three, so no ribbon, no certificate from the WCC (World Chili Congress) to hang on the wall, and no bragging rights.

It may surprise you to know that despite all the promise of award-winning sauces and an appearance on *Joe with the Joes*, that Laurent/Will also failed to find a place among the winners.

We'd later agree, Laurent and I, that the effort we gave toward our entries for the contest was far from our best. We'd just expended too much effort over the day and a half leading up to the contest on making up for lost time and getting to know each other's bodies as intimately as possible.

The Fenimore brothers, out of Midland, Texas, took home top prize, and they probably deserved it, although I do intend to knock their pompous asses off their perch next year.

The joint Laurent and Trey Hale entry ought to be unstoppable.

EPILOGUE

LAURENT

I make Trey promise that he'd let *me* be the one to break the news that he and I got hitched, but he wouldn't be Trey if he wasn't impossible.

After the contest, I sent my assistants back to Knoxville and let *Uncle Waylon's* run itself for a little while. I deserve a vacation anyway, having devoted my every waking hour to building and running the company for the better part of four years.

Trey and I rode on his bike up to Lake Tahoe, where we spent a week in a secluded cabin in the woods unleashing all our years of pent-up sexual frustration on each other, catching up, and talking about the future.

For a variety of reasons, he is anchored to Las Vegas. My business is in Knoxville, but over the past year I'd been resisting overtures from large food conglomerates eager to acquire a young, growing business like mine, so I have options as far as my professional life went. And relocating my business to Las Vegas is another possibility. My key assistants seem game, and Uncle Waylon's sauce and Big Hog BBQ might be a match made in heaven.

My personal life has only one option and desire, which is to spend as much time in close proximity to Trey Hale as humanly possible.

He explains how he is moving the MC away from the illicit activities that generate their cash flow and gradually moving everything financial into the *Hale's Beef, Beer, and Brews* world, and he envisions it is a real possibility over the next few years.

He'll never stop riding, and I'd never want him to. He doesn't want to stop spending time with his brothers, as he sees the *Hale's* chain as an investment vehicle that will allow some of the other Triple U members to pursue their own passions that won't draw the notice of law enforcement.

It's his legacy, and I love his commitment.

Sitting on the porch of that cabin together watching the setting sun, tangled up naked beneath a big blanket, he asks me to marry him. It isn't traditional; he hasn't bought a ring or dropped down on one knee or anything.

It is just a perfect moment for two imperfect people destined to overcome their loss and pain together to fall in love.

I can't say yes fast enough.

We had a party with the MC a week later, but our wedding was a small, simple ceremony on the shore of Lake Tahoe, just the two of us, a minister, and Trey's best friend, Reno, as a witness.

Within a month, we are applying to be foster parents. Fast forward to today, and just last month the wheels are already in motion to adopt our first son. Waylon Tick Hale, a beautiful eighteen month old baby boy. His teenage birth mother had tragically overdosed just weeks after he was born, much like Trey's own mother had done later in life, and we wanted to give him the kind of stable home that neither of us had.

The annual *Sin City Blazin' Hot Chili Cookoff* is right around the corner, with *Hale's* scheduled to host again.

Trey and I have been working together to combine and tweak our recipes, and I have every reason to believe that we'll send the Fenimore brothers back to Texas with their tails between their legs.

Hope to see some of you at *Hale's* for the big show-down. And ladies, there will be plenty of single Triple

U's around if you're into the whole "rugged guys wearing leather and riding Harleys" thing.

Come over and say hello; I'll autograph your bottle of *Uncle Waylon's*.

Maybe I can play matchmaker.

Be the first to find out about all of Dillon Hart's new releases, book sales, and freebies by joining his VIP Mailing List. Join today and get a FREE book -- instantly! Join by clicking here!

ABOUT THE AUTHOR

Dillon Hart, who lives in San Francisco, writes compelling gay romance novels that embody the essence of love and human relationships. His works are inspired by the diverse communities that call the city home, from the vibrant Castro neighborhood to the bohemian Mission district. In his spare time, Dillon enjoys riding the F Line streetcar from Market Street to Fisherman's Wharf, where he enjoys the ocean breezes and the bustle of the waterfront.

More on www.dillonhart.com

Join my newsletter by clicking here.

Write me at contact@dillonhart.com

FIND ME ON SOCIAL MEDIA

Milton Keynes UK
Ingram Content Group UK Ltd.
UKHW020724301023
431584UK00014B/624